ACADEMY FOR ROBLOX PROS

AN UNOFFICIAL ROBLOX GRAPHIC NOVEL

Scholastic Australia
An imprint of Scholastic Australia Pty Limited
PO Box 579 Gosford NSW 2250
ABN 11 000 614 577
www.scholastic.com.au

Part of the Scholastic Group
Sydney • Auckland • New York • Toronto • London • Mexico City • New Delhi
• Hong Kong • Buenos Aires • Puerto Rico

Published by Scholastic Australia in 2024.
Written and illustrated by Louis Shea.

NATIONAL LIBRARY OF AUSTRALIA

A catalogue record for this book is available from the National Library of Australia

ISBN: 978-1-76129-965-0

Typeset in Extra Crunchy.

Printed in China by Hang Tai Printing Company Limited.

Scholastic Australia's policy, in association with Hang Tai, is to use papers that are renewable and made efficiently from wood grown in responsibly managed sources, so as to minimise its environmental footprint.

10 9 8 7 6 5 4 3 2 24 25 26 27 28 / 2

ACADEMY FOR ROBLOX PROS

AN UNOFFICIAL ROBLOX GRAPHIC NOVEL

As the sun rises on another beautiful school day, all is quiet and peaceful, until . . .

Bea's House
BZZZZT!
BZZZZT!
Beatrice! It's time to get up!
Nooo!
Mitch's House
BEEP!
BEEP!
7:00
You need to get ready for school, Mitch!
Uh ...
Who ...
What ...
When ...

Tash's House
DING! DING!
No more sleeping in, Tash!
Just another 10 minutes ...

Jai's House
BRRRT! BRRRT! BRRRT!
Jai! Wake up!
ZZZZZZZZZ

Hurry up! What are you doing in there?
SQUEAK!
Keep an eye on the time, Mitch!
WHRRR!
BZZZZ!
Tash! Let someone else use the bathroom!
FWOOSH!
Huh?
Are you awake yet, Jai?!
SQUELCH!

You better hurry, or you'll be late!
I don't hurry.
Make sure you get to school on time.
I'm always on time, Mum.
Bye darling! Have a good ...
Bye! Gotta fly!
Jai! You've forgotten your shoes ... again!

Wait up, Tash!
Hey, Bea! Hey, Mitch! Have I made it in time?
Yep, the bus will be here in exactly one minute.
BUS STOP
Really...?

'Cause it looks like it's already come and gone!
STOP
VROOOM!

Oh no! I'm going to be late!
I knew I should have stayed in bed.
Maybe we could run to the next bus stop?
We'll never get there before it, unless ...

Shortcut time! Follow me!
C'mon guys!
Ugh! Do we have to run?

BZZZzz!
TIK!
TIK!
WOOF!
GRRR!
WOOF!

There's the bus stop!
And there's the bus!
We've missed it again!
Not if I can help it!
BROOOM!
Stop the bus!
I command you to ...

... stop ...
SCREEECH!
... the ...
WHOOSH!
OOF!
SCH
SPLAT!

Nice work, Jai!
Thno pwoblem ...
Are you okay, Jai?
I think I can see the back of my brain ...
Don't worry, we'll be at school soon. You'll be able to give your brain a rest there!

ROBLOX PRO PROFILES

Name: Beatrice
Favourite subject: Art
Most hated subject: P.E.
Likes: Loud music
Dislikes: Loud people
Special skills: Rolling her eyes

Name: Mitch
Favourite subject: Science
Most hated subject: Music
Likes: Knowing how things work
Dislikes: Decision making
Special skills: Electronics

Name: Tash
Favourite subject: P.E.
Most hated subject: English
Likes: Sports
Dislikes: Messy hair
Special skills: Kicking things hard

Name: Jai
Favourite subject: Lunch break
Most hated subject: History, maths, geography ...
Likes: Food
Dislikes: Celery
Special skills: Making Hamdoza's (a combination of hamburger, hot dogs and pizza)

BORELOCK'S ACADEMY

Borelock's Academy is a ~~proud~~ . . . ~~noble~~ . . . ~~prestigious~~ old institution that was founded by the Borelock family long ago.

Originally starting out as slug farmers, the Borelock family soon realised that no-one really wanted to eat slugs . . . or keep them as pets, so they decided instead to build a school.

Since then, Borelock's Academy has educated many generations of children on the joys of slugs and other less interesting stuff.

The current principal, Warren Borelock, proudly continues his ancestors' love of slugs and ~~hatred~~. . . *tolerance* of children.

As he can often be heard muttering, 'They might be slimy and horrible, but someone's got to teach them!'

But Borelock's Academy is not just all about fun and slugs. There are plenty of other exciting classes, too! There's science . . .

And English . . .

Fun outdoor sports, and ~~music~~ noise making!

Urgh ... Braaain ... Sore brain!
Is your head still hurting, Jai?
You probably should see someone about that ...
What? No, my head's fine.
I just had *double* History!
Ah, that would explain it.

What do you want to do for the rest of lunchtime?
There's nothing to do! It's pouring outside.
We could go to the computer lab and play Roblox?
I wish! The school computers are sooo slow!
Yeah, they're dog water.
I might have a way to fix that. I've put together a little device that should solve our problems!

Are you sure this will work, Mitch?
It's just a matter of making sure that the wave functions of ...
A simple 'yes' or 'no' will do.

Well, let's find out!

Bing!

It's working, Mitch! You're a genius!
I'm going to create a new avatar!
Me too! One with fantastic hair!
Hmm ... maybe I'll choose the ... no ...
Now, what shall I call myself?

What about ... no ... umm ...
SLURP!
What are you dweebs doing?!
Isn't there somewhere else you should be, Roger?
Like a swamp, or lurking under a bridge?
Huh?

Meanwhile, in his office, Principal Borelock is having trouble loading his favourite 'watching paint dry' website.
What's going on?!
LOADING
CLICK! CLICK!
Tap! Tap!

Argh! I was just getting to the exciting second coat!
Something must have happened to the internet.

SLAM!
I'll get to the bottom of this!

Back in the lab ...
Shove over and give me a go!
SHOVE!
Go away, Roger!
Now look what you've done!
That was your fault! You owe me a super slime slushie!

It's ruined!
CRACKLE!
TCHKT!
CRACK!
Uh-oh!
CRACKLE!
TCHKT!
KRRRKT!

As Mitch's device malfunctioned, the computer lab was plunged into darkness.

'Nice one, Roger!' snapped Bea.

'I didn't do anything' replied Roger. 'Mitch made me . . .'

'How about we stop fighting and try and find a way out of here instead?' said Tash. 'There should be an exit sign somewhere . . .'

But the kids, stumbling and bumbling in the pitch black, couldn't find the door anywhere.

Panic started to set in as Roger became more and more hysterical.

'We're trapped!' he wailed. 'We're all going to die in here! I'm running out of air . . . need oxygen . . . Help! Help! Heeeelp!!!'

'I don't think there's any help for him!' muttered Bea.

'We've got to get out of here soon!' stammered Mitch. 'We'll be late for class!'

At that moment, an eerie green light began glowing in the corner of the room. An outline of a doorway, with a sign above it, slowly became visible.

'There you go,' said Jai. 'No need to panic at all. I knew we'd find the exit . . .'

But the sign read 'enter', not 'exit', and as they watched, a strange square shape appeared in front of them.

Trembling a little, the kids approached the glowing door and opened it . . .

ENTER
Careful, Jai!
Whoa!

What is that?!
I don't know, and I don't want to find out!
Me neither! Let's find the proper exit and get out of here!

What?! And go back to class? No way! Let's go!
SHOVE!
Roger!!!

CREATING AVATARS . . .
Huh?
What's happening to me?!
Argh! My hair!

My face! My beautiful face!
My butt! My beautiful bu ...

WELCOME, GLITCH.
WELCOME, BEE.
WELCOME, PLAY.

What's happened to us?
CLUNK!
Well, it's obvious, isn't it?

WELCOME, DASH.
WELCOME, OGRE.
Oof!
THWUMP!
Maybe to you, Mitch, but not to me!
I didn't say anything ...

Then who was it?
It was me!
EEEK! Get it off me!
Calm down, Glitch! I'm not an 'it', I'm your hair!

Cool! Talking hair!
So that's where he keeps his extra big brain of his!
And it explains why he's always in two minds about everything!
So what's happened, Mitc— sorry, Glitch's hair?
Call me Fritz! Well, we've been turned into Roblox avatars.
Well yeah, but how?
That I'm actually not sure about ...
I bet it was Roger's fault!

If it was, it's the best thing he's ever done!
This is awesome!
Check out these sweet avatar moves!
Can't pick my nose though ...
Donk! Donk!
Um, you don't have a nose.
Oh, yeah ...

You should thank me, dweebs! If it wasn't for me, we'd still be in that stupid computer room! Or worse ... in class!

It's good to see the game got your avatar right ... Ogre!
Whatever, Bug! You're just jealous I've got a club!
I guess it'd be useful to scratch your butt with.
Huh?
Ooh ... that's good!
Scritch! Scritch!
Ewww! Gross!
I wish I had a club.

Hey guys! Some arrows have appeared on the floor. I think we're meant to follow them.
Oh ... I don't know ...

Stop overthinking, Glitch, and listen to your hair! Let's go!

ROBLOX AVATAR PROFILES

Beatrice's avatar name: Bee
Though her avatar doesn't have an actual sting, Bee's sharp comebacks more than make up for this!

Mitch's avatar name: Glitch

Mitch's hair's avatar name: Fritz
As his friends pointed out, Glitch's ample brain is always in two minds! Fritz has all the confidence and is ready to guide Glitch and his friends in the Roblox universe!

Tash's avatar name: Dash
Just like in the real world, Dash loves to move! She's ready for any obby Roblox throws at her!

Jai's avatar name: Play
Play by name, Play by nature! Always ready for fun, Play will sometimes learn stuff too!

Roger's avatar name: Ogre
Being a true coward (like his real life self), Ogre hides his fear behind his 'tough' monstrous green avatar appearance... and his club.

The avatars followed the green arrows until they reached a door with another 'Enter' sign above it.

'Not another one!' said Glitch. 'I think we should turn back. Who knows what's on the other side?!'

'Whatever it is, it'll be better than school!' replied Ogre.

'I hate to agree with Ogre, but I think he's right, Glitch,' said Play. 'Look, there's a sign on the door. Let's see what it says at least.'

Under the heading 'Bus Run', was a description of a challenge that needed to be completed to go any further in the game.

ENTER
BUS
RUN

Bus run? What's that about?
It says here that to complete the challenge you have to catch the 'Academy for Roblox Pros' bus.
BUS RUN
Catch a bus?! That is sooo EASY! Not much of a challenge!
You dweebs found it hard enough this morning!

HA HA
HA HA
HA!
Well I'm not waiting for Ogre to push me through this time! Play is right, how hard could it be to catch a ...

... bus.

I think we'll need to split up to find it.
How are we going to keep in touch?
Easy!
We'll use a chatbox ...
Fritz: Like this!
Play: Cool!
Bee: Good one Fritz!
Dash: Great idea!
Glitch: I would have thought of this too ...
Fritz: Don't be jealous, Glitch.

BLOX CITY
Fritz: Any luck yet?
Dash: Not yet!
Ogre: Help!! A bus is trying to eat me!
Glitch: As if! If you're not going to help, Ogre, just keep quiet!
DINO EXPRESS
Bee: OMG! Forget the academy. I've found a much better bus!
Dash: Focus, Bee!
Bee: But they're so cute!

SUCKER XPRESS
Play: Um ... do any of you have some garlic ... or a stake?!
Glitch: Now's not the time to be thinking about eating, Play!
Dash: Glitch, how are you and Fritz going? Have you seen the bus yet?
Glitch: Maybe ... I think I saw ... no ... could that be one ... um ...
Fritz: Stop spinning so fast, Glitch! I think I'm going to be sick . . .
SPACE BLOX

Bee: Awesome! I see it!
Glitch: Well done, Dash! I was starting to think we'd never find it!
Fritz: Excellent work! And may I say, what wonderful hair you have!
Ogre: Ha ha! Fritz has a crush on Dash's hair!
Fritz: I do not! I was just remarking on how well it looked when the light was shining off her flowing, glossy ...
Glitch: Shhh, Fritz! You're making it worse!
Bee: Um, when you're all finished, maybe we should get on the bus before it leaves?
Fritz: Good idea Bee ... all aboard!
Dash: Where's Play?

STOP! Wait for ...
SCREEECH!
Me! OOF!
Swish!
SPLAT!
FANKS ...
You're getting good at stopping buses, Play!
Oooh ... do I have five hands now ...?

I wonder what the Academy for Roblox Pros is like?

Can't be any worse than Borelock's Academy!
I bet it's super cool!

Super *lame* is more like it!
It's a school! There's no cool in school!
Well, actually ...
Hey guys, look!
Cool school!
Really cool!
Super cool!
Coolius Maximus!
Coolest!

ACADEMY FOR ROBLOX PROS
A
R

The Academy for Roblox Pros is not your average school! While it does have the usual school things—classes, teachers, students, jocks, nerds, scary librarians . . . that's where the similarities end!

It was founded by Principal Blox who was one of the original Roblox avatars—and he still sports the retro blocky old-school look!

Principal Blox wanted to create a school where new players could learn the ways of Roblox and where experienced avatars could level-up their skills.

Using action-packed simulations, puzzles, role playing and obbys, the school teaches students to use problem solving and teamwork as they learn and explore in the Roblox universe.

It's the only school where students want to do their homework!

WORLD'S
BLOCKIEST
PRINCIPAL

What do we do now?
Let's ask someone.
Excuse me, we were wondering ...
Ha! More noobs, hey?
Um ... yeah ... could you tell us ...
I don't think so, noob! You're not getting Boosted Ape from us!

Charming.
What's Boosted Ape?
I like these guys!
Later, noobs!
I think I'm going to get sick of that word pretty soon!
BING! BING!
ATTENTION NEW STUDENTS
This morning's classes will be as follows:
• Science
Yes!
• Music
Awesome!
• History
Oh!
• P.E.
I can't wait!

LESSON 1—SCIENCE
Find the T-rex eggs . . . before the T-rex finds you!
CRACK!

LESSON 2—MUSIC
Jump to the beat!
TSSK!
BOOM!
PLING!
PLONG!

LESSON 3—HISTORY
Escape Captain Bloxbeard and his pirate crew!

LESSON 4—P.E.
Score the goal before the ball explodes!
KABOOM!
FzzzZzzZZ!

What a morning! Who knew learning could be so fun?

I know! Riding dinosaurs in science, escaping pirates in history ... even you must have enjoyed that, Pla–

Where's Play gone?
He was here a second ago ... I hope he's okay!
Hey, guys! Check this out!
Play! What have you got?!

Oh, just a little bit of lunch.
You're a computer game avatar, Play ... the food's not real!
Nom! Nom!
Mmmm!

Nom!
Nom!
mmmm!
That's delicious! Gimme more!
Oi! Get your own!

A tasty time later ...
BING! BING!
BURP!
Lunch's over. We'd better get to the next class.
Nom! Nom!
I think it's maths.
Look! It's those jocks from this morning ... seems like they're bullying someone else now!
?
BRAINS
BRAINS

Brains?! Do you think they've lost theirs?
They must be serving them at the canteen! Maybe I should get some ...
Gross. Play!
They looked a bit green, didn't they?
Maybe they're not feeling well ...
Do you think you can be sick in Roblox?

Can you get sick in Roblox?

Is that what a computer virus is?

Could Maths ever be fun?

Could you get brains at the canteen?

And if so, what did they taste like?!

These, and many other questions, were discussed by the gang, as they headed excitedly off to their next class. But behind them, storm clouds were brewing at the Academy for Roblox Pros. Students were beginning to behave strangely . . . well, more strangely than usual.

How do I get off this thing?!
Help! This equation's gone feral!
G+R+R×R=!

FINISH
And the answer is ...
42
Pi?! What sort of pie? Raspberry?
ROBLOXI·AE

CONGRATULATIONS, GLITCH. YOU SCORED 100% ON THE TEST.
FINISH
SWISH!
42

Well done, Glitch!
I couldn't do it without you, Fritz!

Stop it! You're making me blush!
SCREECH!
There's Ms Fractal. I wonder what we're doing now?
We've finished the test, Ms Fractal!
And we got 100%!
100%? Well done. That must *moan* ... mean you have a very big, juicy ...

BRAINS!

BRAIN!
BRAINS!

Meanwhile, Play, Dash and Bee were having problems of their own . . .

'Where's Glitch when you need him?!' shouted Play as he dived out of the way of another killer equation.

'I don't know,' replied Bee warily as she eyed two hungry sums that were approaching from the shadows.

'I think we'll just have to do this without the help of Glitch's big brain,' said Dash. 'Let's team up and get out of here! Play, you take down that multiplication table. Bee, you deal with that sneaky statistic creeping up behind us and I'm going to kick this fraction in the denominator!'

I always knew maths was dangerous!
I'm just glad I passed!
That was the worst pie ever!

I wonder how Glitch did?
Aced it, I bet.
Yeah, he's probably getting some award from the teacher.

Whoa! What's happened here? Where is everyone?
BRAINS
BRAINS
BRAINS
BRAINS
BRAINS
BRAINS
BRAINS

This is super eerie!
There's no-one around.
If only! Look who's headed our way!

What's up, noobs?
GRRRR!
Ogre, do you know what's happened to everyone?
They probably saw you coming and ran away!
Ha! Ha! Ha! Ha! Ha!
Yyyeah ... ha ... ha. Seriously though, this is getting ...
CLICK!
Creepy!

And for the second time that day, the avatars were plunged into darkness.

'You didn't spill another slushie, did you, Ogre?' asked Play.

'Oh ha ha,' sneered Ogre. 'For your information, it wasn't my fault, it was Glitch who pushed me over—'

'Shhh!' whispered Dash. 'I think I can hear something . . .'

Eventually, after a lot of muttering from Ogre, they all fell silent. As they did, they became aware of a low moaning sound all around them.

Slowly, the noise got closer and louder.

GROAN!
MOAN!
GROAN!

What is it?
GROAN!
Sounds like we're back in maths!
MOAN!

We're not going to be able to find anything out in the dark. Let's see if we can find a light switch.

Is this it?
I think I've found it ...
Ouch!
That's my face!
Oops! Sorry!
CLICK!
Success! Light!
Um guys ... I've found out what's making the noise ...

ZOMBIES!

MOAN!
GROAN!
BRAINS!
BRAINS!
BRAINS!

Alright ... don't panic! If we stick together we might be oka–
Ogre!
EEEEEEEEEEEK!
Huh?
The zombies are ignoring him!

Probably because they're after brains!
Or because he's green and drools!
Guys! They may be ignoring Ogre ...

But not us! Run!!
BRAINS!
MOAN!

ZOMBIES

ZOMBIE STATS

- **Speed:** Slow, but persistent.
- **Attack:** Will try to snack on your brains. Wearing a helmet when hanging out with a zombie is advisable.
- **Colour:** They range from light snot to dark pond-scum green.
- **Smell:** A mixture of bins, rotten fish and unwashed gym socks.
- **Likes:** Brains, moaning, Irish dancing.
- **Dislikes:** Joggers.

HINT:

How to spot a zombie

It can be extremely difficult to tell the difference between a zombie and a normal student. Both moan, drool and smell of decay. A giveaway is that zombies are more interested in brains . . . and they're a bit greener.

While Bee, Dash and Play were running away from the zombies, Glitch was walking and moaning with his new green buddies.

But Fritz, still in a state of shock, wasn't so keen to be going with the flow!

When Ms Fractal attacked them at the end of Maths, she hadn't taken notice of Fritz and had only turned Glitch into a mindless ghoul!

Fritz was saved, but now he had no choice but to follow the zombie horde.

This is going from bad to worse! thought Fritz.

If only I could escape and get help ... I don't think Glitch feels like a haircut though . . .

As the zombie mass moved on, Fritz tried desperately to come up with a plan.

Firstly, I need to stop Glitch from following the rest of the zombies. I don't know where they're going, but I can't imagine it's good! All this moaning and saying brains is giving me the shivers . . . and who is this master they keep talking about? I have to see if I can get through to Glitch . . .

GROAN!
Psst, Glitch! It's me, Fritz. You've got to snap out of it, buddy!
BRAINS!
Brains?
Oh, um ... moan ... brraaains!

Phew! That was close. I'll have to be more careful from now on.

Where are we going?

KRRAAACK!
MAASTER!

Welcome, my pretties! It is I, *The Warlock*, your master!

I have taken over the academy, and with your help, will soon ...

... be the ruler of all of Roblox!
Oh no!

You won't get away with this!
RATTLE!
SHAKE!
Oh yes, I will! And now that I've turned you into a zombie as well, you'll help me!
ZAP!
Now go, my faithful green army, and find students who've escaped!

GROAN!
BRAINS!
MOAN!
SLAM!
Man, those zombies just don't give up!

MOAN!
GROAN!
We can't keep running! There's too many of them!
Maybe we could find somewhere to hide ...?
THUMP!
THUMP!
THUMP!

‘I’ve got it!’ said Bee. ‘We can’t run, and we can’t hide, but we can disguise! Follow me!’ she shouted, and raced off down the corridor. Play and Dash followed as Bee led them to the Roblox art room.

‘I don’t think now’s the time for painting,’ panted Play.

‘That depends what you’re painting,’ replied Bee with a grin.

Into the classroom they went, and Bee began looking through the art supplies.

As a bewildered Dash and Play watched on, Bee found some cans of green paint and three brushes.

'Right,' she said, 'Time to blend in.'

But Dash and Play were still confused.

'We're going to paint ourselves to look like zombies!' snapped Bee. 'You both have the right expressions for a zombie at the moment, now put on the paint before they find us!'

What do you think, Bee?
Here, let me help!
Much better!
Thanks ...

Yo! Check out my sweet disguise!
I'm Count Blocula!

We're disguising ourselves as zombies, Play. Not vampires!
Oh! But vampires are way cooler ...
Put on the paint, Play!

Looking good! Now it's time to release our inner zombies!
Wow, Bee! You're a natural!
GROAN! MOAN!
Shuffle!
It's easy! You just need to channel Ogre!
BRAINS!
Nice drooling, Dash!

GROAN!
BRAINS!
RAAARGH!
Um ... maybe dial the zombie down a bit ...?
?
TSSST!
MOAN!
Okay guys, here they come! Time to join the horde!

Cautiously, they edged out of the classroom and joined onto the back of the marching zombies. At first, they were terrified they'd be found out, but as they kept going, their confidence rose. The zombies seemed to accept them as their own!

'I can't believe it's working,' mumbled Play. 'What do we do now?'

'Let's just see where they're going and . . . look!' Bee exclaimed, pointing ahead. 'I think that's . . . Yes! It looks like Glitch!'

'Oh no!' cried Dash. 'He's a zombie!'

'Yeah . . .' said Play hesitantly, 'But he's still got hair . . . like us. Maybe he's pretending too?'

'Or he's only part zombie . . . can you be part zombie?' asked Dash.

'We need to get him away from the rest of the zombies and find out,' said Bee. 'But how?'

'Leave that to me,' said Play as he began shouldering his way through the mass of green.

MOAN! GROAN!
Coming through. BRAINS!
Official zombie business! GROAN!
Watch it, dribbles!
BRAINS!
MOAN!
Shove!

MOAN!
You, zombie with funny hair! Master see you now!
GROAN!
BRAINS?

Nice one, Play!
What now?!
Hey guys! It's me, Fritz! I'm so glad to see you!
Fritz! You're okay! What happened to Glitch?
Ms Fractal turned him into a zombie at the end of maths!
Woah! That's harsh! I'm glad she didn't see what I got in the test!
Don't worry about that! I've found out who's behind it all ...

Fritz told them about the Warlock and how he had a magic staff that could transform avatars into zombies. He then explained Warlock's fiendish plan to take over the school and then unleash his zombie army on the rest of Roblox.

'We have to stop him!' exclaimed Dash.

'Yeah,' agreed Play 'This is the best school ever! I'm not letting this Warlock ruin everything!'

'We have to find a way to get that staff off him,' said Bee. 'If it can turn avatars into zombies, then it can probably turn them back.'

Bee, Play, Dash and Fritz, intent on saving the school and their friend Glitch, set about formulating a way to take down the Warlock. A little later, they had the beginnings of a cunning plan . . .

'I think it might just work' said Fritz. 'But I'm not going to be able to help you at all . . . Unfortunately, zombie Glitch has a mind of his own!'

At that moment, the kids heard a muffled, whimpering noise. They crept cautiously towards the sound and found Ogre, curled up and shaking in the corner of the room.

'Aargh! Zombies!' he screamed as he saw them. 'Please don't eat my brains!'

'It's okay, Ogre' said Dash soothingly 'It's us, Bee, Play and Dash. We're only disguised as zombies. No-one's going to eat your brains!'

'Wouldn't be much of a meal, anyway,' sniggered Bee.

'N . . nn . . . not zombies?' He snivelled. 'What are you doing then?'

'We're going to save the school!' said Play. 'And you're going to help us!'

So, everyone know what to do?
BRAINS?
Yep, we're ready to take this Warlock and his zombie minions down!

Uh-oh!
Zombie Glitch is getting mad! I think he's realised something's up!
BRAINS! BRAINS!

Quick! Get started before he finds the Warlock! Good luck!
MASTER!
STOMP! STOMP!

Right, guys! Let's save Glitch!
And the Academy!
And Roblox!
And me!

ATTENTION ZOMBIE HORDE! The Master has made a series of games for you to compete in ... to see which of you ... will become ... the Top Zombie!
First up, we have ...

DANCING WITH THE SCARS
What a moanwalk! Using his own drool to help smooth his slide is inspired!
SLOOP!
Onto Brainroom dancing ... and what a lovely couple these two ghouls make!
OOF!
It's now time for the Zomba! Part dance, part exercise and all fun! Just watch out for the flying limbs!

Next up ...
THE GREAT ZOMBIE BAKE OFF!
There's strong competition today! Just look at that delicious Brainberry Sneeze cake!
ACHOO!
Uh-oh! Looks like we have a bit of trouble here with one of the contestants! Their Baked Brain Alaska is turning into more of a Flambé Zombé.

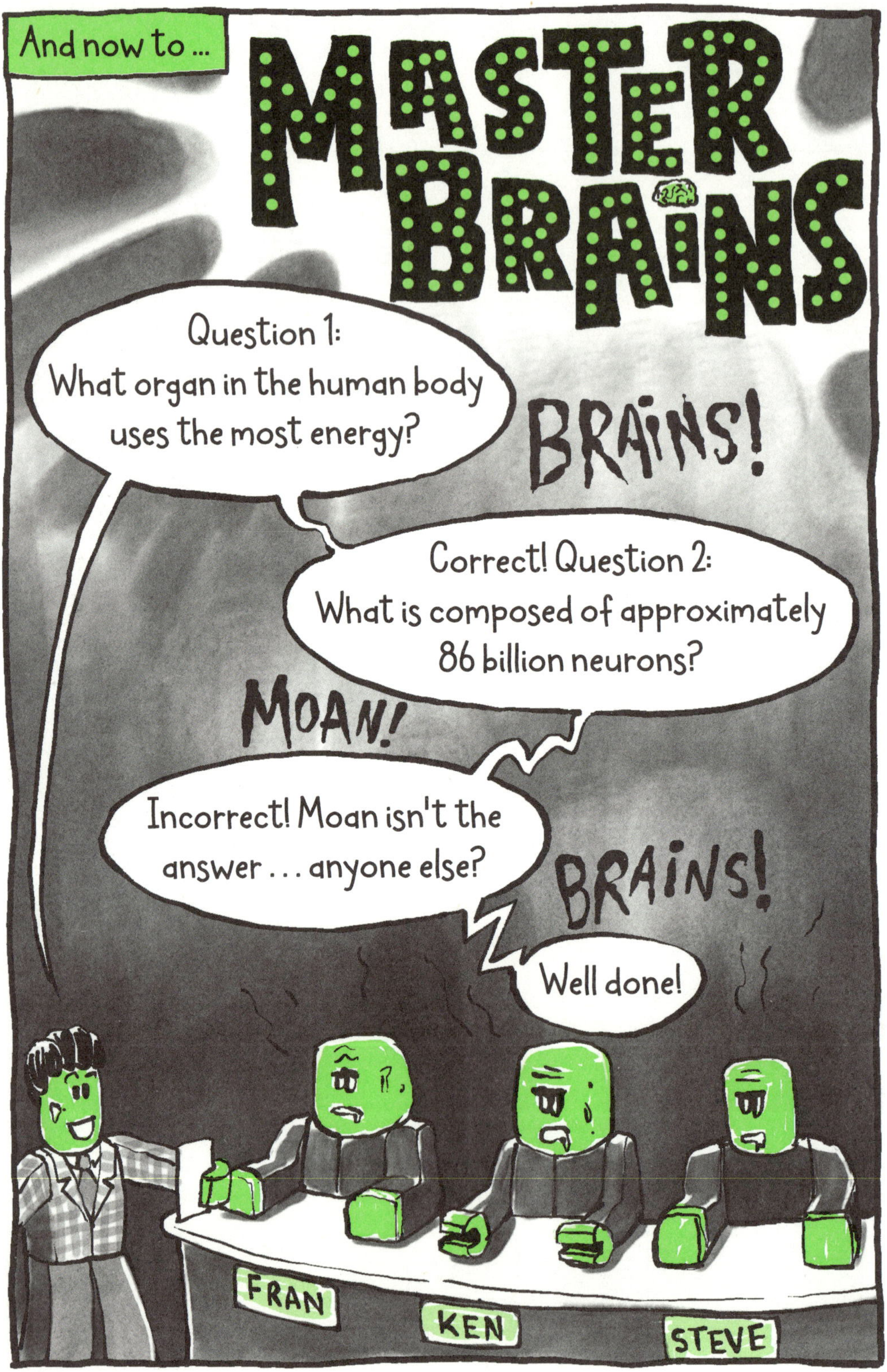
And now to ...
MASTER BRAINS
Question 1:
What organ in the human body uses the most energy?
BRAINS!
Correct! Question 2:
What is composed of approximately 86 billion neurons?
MOAN!
Incorrect! Moan isn't the answer . . . anyone else?
BRAINS!
Well done!
FRAN
KEN
STEVE

What's going on?!
Stop, you foolish zombies!!! Obey me or ...
CLICK!
Huh?
Welcome to ...

ROBLOX IDOL
BRAINS!
GROAN!
CLAP!

WHOOO!
CHEER!

Your name, please?
What? Um ... It's Warlock ... The Warlock.
The Warlock?! Hmmm, a little bit cliché, isn't it?
Tss Tss He he he!
And what makes you think you can win Roblox Idol?

Well ... um ... ever since I was a small blox ... sorry, boy, I've dreamed of becoming a powerful wizard who *sob* takes over the whole world! *sob*

Oh ... er ... what a touching story. Well, once you've pulled yourself together, show us what you've got!
Sob!

I can fly!
SWOOSH!

And control the weather!
KABOOM!!

Or grow into a GIANT!

Well. It's a no from me.
And me ... Play! What are you doing?
What?! I thought he was pretty good!
You can't be serious! You wouldn't know talent if it zapped you with a magic wand ... now, there's a thought!
The magic wand is the problem! It seems to have all the talent. I bet you've got no skills without it!

Oh yeah!
Check this out!
CLUNK!
DONK!
MOAN!
Um ... ace of spa ...
no wait ... four
of hearts!
GROAN!

And now for the grand finale! I shall pull a ...

... rabbit from a hat!
Got it!

My staff! Give that to me!
Sure thing! Here you are!
ZAP!
SQUEAK!
Ooh!! This is fun!
ZAP!
ZAP!
ZAP!

Well done, Ogre!
Quick! Use it on the zombies!
Huh?

I don't think so! Now that I have the staff, I control the zombies! Now I'll be the ruler of Roblox!

Give that here!
SNATCH!
What is it with everyone wanting to take over the world?!
Um ... Bee ...
BRAINS!
Zombies!

ZAP!

All done!
Not yet! Here comes Glitch!
BRAINS!

ZAP!

Hey guys!
How did you go in the maths test?
Why are you painted green?
It's good to have you back, Glitch!
Though you did make a pretty good zombie!
Yeah! You were terrifying!
Zombie?! What are you talking about?

After a quick dip in the school pool, to get rid of their remnant zombie green colouring, the kids were then summoned by Principal Blox to an assembly.

'Each of you has shown extraordinary bravery and creativity today, and in doing so, you have saved our beloved academy,' the Principal said. 'As a small token of my, and indeed all the school's appreciation, it gives me great pleasure to give you these'. He handed each of them a small badge in the shape of a school crest. 'These badges mean that you are now, officially, members of the Academy for Roblox Pros!' The school burst into applause and cheering.

'These badges will help you travel back to your own world and, more importantly, return here so you can continue your learning at this academy.'

Another loud round of applause drowned out the cheers and whoops of joy from Play, Bee, Dash, Ogre, Glitch and Fritz at this news.

These badges are awesome!
Useful and stylish!
Nice work, noo ... new kids.
Yeah, not bad for your first day.
Praise from those guys?! This academy just keeps on surprising me!
BING!
There goes the bell.
School's over ... I guess it's time to go home.

Principal Blox said the badges will glow and we'll be transported back.
Oh! Do we have to?
Here goes!
See you back in the real wo ...

...oooorld!

ENTER
EXIT
BING!
WHOOSH!
Woah!
THUD!
Oof!

I don't think I'll ever get used to that!
Arrgh! My hair!
Pat! Pat!
I miss my fantastic Roblox hair!
Still, it's nice to have fingers again!
Jai! Gross!
Pick! Pick!

Oh no! We're going to be in so much trouble! We were in the game for ages! What are the teachers going to say?! What are my parents going to say?!

Relax, Mitch! Lunch isn't even over yet.

Phew!
I guess time is different in Roblox.
Oh! I don't want to go back to class.

Well, I'm off! See you losers tomorrow ...
... and don't expect me to save you noobs again!
Noobs?!
RAAARGH!

Do you think we should stop Bea?

Nah, Roger's had it coming for a while! Let's get back to class.

Tash, Mitch, Jai and (eventually) Bea headed back to class, and not even the thought of double Maths could dampen their spirits.

They knew that soon they would be returning to the Academy for Roblox Pros, where they'd have lots of exciting adventures, make new friends . . . and see what else there was to get in the canteen.

Having battled The Warlock and his zombie minions, they knew that together they could face anything, and overcome any obstacle . . . except maybe getting the bus on time.

Later that night ...
EXIT
CLUNK!
CRASH!
BOOM!
SQUEAK!
AAARGH!
Blast! Back in this dump!
Well, at least I managed to get one of these!

Mwa Ha Ha Ha Ha Haa!!!
Te he he he!

ACADEMY FOR ROBLOX PROS

BOOK 2 COMING SOON!